NUGGET & FANG

Tammi Sauer   Michael Slack

SCHOLASTIC INC.

D1031022

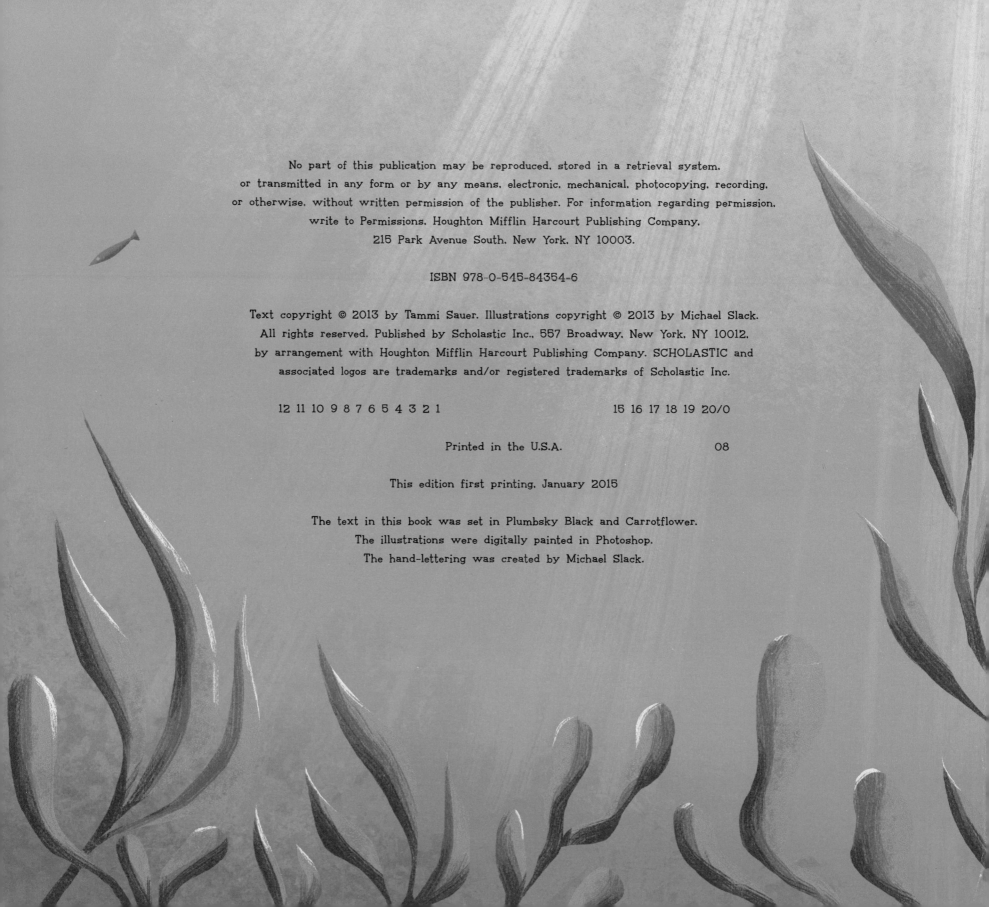

No part of this publication may be reproduced, stored in a retrieval system,
or transmitted in any form or by any means, electronic, mechanical, photocopying, recording,
or otherwise, without written permission of the publisher. For information regarding permission,
write to Permissions, Houghton Mifflin Harcourt Publishing Company,
215 Park Avenue South, New York, NY 10003.

ISBN 978-0-545-84354-6

Text copyright © 2013 by Tammi Sauer. Illustrations copyright © 2013 by Michael Slack.
All rights reserved. Published by Scholastic Inc., 557 Broadway, New York, NY 10012,
by arrangement with Houghton Mifflin Harcourt Publishing Company. SCHOLASTIC and
associated logos are trademarks and/or registered trademarks of Scholastic Inc.

12 11 10 9 8 7 6 5 4 3 2 1   15 16 17 18 19 20/0

Printed in the U.S.A.   08

This edition first printing, January 2015

The text in this book was set in Plumbsky Black and Carrotflower.
The illustrations were digitally painted in Photoshop.
The hand-lettering was created by Michael Slack.

For the fang-tastic Mason and Bryant—T.S.

For Nola Belle—M.S.

In the deep, deep ocean
lived two best friends.
Nugget and Fang.
They did everything together.

They swam over.
GLUG

They swam under.
GLUG-GLUG

BOO!

They swam all around.
GLUG-GLUG-GLUG

Life was close to perfect . . .

until it was time for Nugget to go to school.

STOP

MINI MINNOWS

Welcome
to a brand
New Year

On Monday, Nugget was busy with . . .

READING

"Today's story is about three little minnows and a big, bad shark . . ."

"A big, *bad* shark?
Ha!" said Nugget. "Impossible."

THE
THREE LITTLE
MINNOWS

Nugget was busy with . . .

MATH

$$1 + 1 = 2$$
$$2 + 2 = 4$$

But what if there were ten minnows and a shark came along and ate four of them?

How many minnows are left?

"Is this a trick question? A shark would never do that!" said Nugget.

And Nugget was busy with . . .

SCIENCE

"Sharks are scary. Here's the proof!"

MARINE FOOD CHAIN

SHARK

"The stuff on that poster isn't true," said Nugget.
"My best *friend* is a shark!"

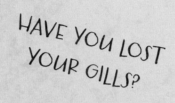

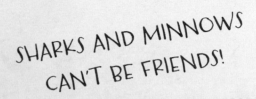

HAVE YOU LOST
YOUR GILLS?

SHARKS AND MINNOWS
CAN'T BE FRIENDS!

HELLO—SHARKS EAT MINNOWS!

Nugget was shocked. (And apparently delicious.)

That afternoon, Nugget explained it all to Fang.
"Sharks are toothy. Sharks are scary.
Sharks and minnows can't be friends."

NUGGET

Food Chain Test

1. Sharks eat:

A+

a. Minnows
b. Rusty license plates
c. Surfers
d. All of the above

"Sounds fishy to me," said Fang.
"It's true. See?" said Nugget.
He held up his test.
Then he swam far, far away.

Fang's heart sank.
There was nothing he could do about being toothy.

But he needed his best buddy back.
He had to prove he wasn't scary.

On Tuesday, Mini Minnows had a surprise visitor.
A very BIG surprise visitor.

The visitor gave Nugget his friendliest smile.

SHARK!
SWIM FOR
YOUR LIVES!

"Oh, my algae!" said Nugget. "It's Fang."

On Wednesday, Fang tried a different approach.

HE WANTS

TO EAT

YOU

FOR

"Holy mackerel!" said Nugget.

DINNER!

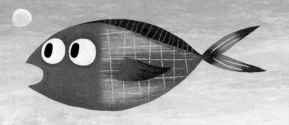

On Thursday, Fang tried everything he could think of.

A tattoo.

A special delivery.

YOU'RE FINTASTIC

A song and dance.

But nothing worked.

On Friday, Fang was out of ideas.

All alone, he swam over.
BLUB

He swam under.
BLUB-BLUB

He swam all around.
BLUB-BLUB-THWUMP

Life was not even close to perfect.

Fang was so busy boo-hooing,
he didn't notice a net drop

down,

down,

down . . .

right on the mini minnows!

OH, NO!

The net pulled up, **up, up.**

SOMEBODY, HELP!

Fang squinted. "Nugget?"
He had to do something. But what?

Fang fanned his gills.
He wrung his fins. Then . . .

PING!

Fang had a plan.

Fang's big sharp teeth chomped.
Fang's big sharp teeth chewed.

Fang saved the mini minnows!

All the minnows stared.

"I know, I know," said Fang.
"I'm toothy. Too scary. Too . . . shark."

WAIT!

Nugget swam toward Fang.
"There were ten minnows," he said, "and a very special shark came along. How many friends are there altogether?"

There was only one answer.

In the deep, deep ocean lived eleven friends.

They swam over.
GLUG

They swam under.
GLUG-GLUG

They swam all around.
GLUG-GLUG-GLUG

And everyone was all smiles.
Especially you-know-who.